Ya'll Won't Let Me Sing

Chapter One

Francoise

Ya'll Won't Let Me Sing
Chapter One

Copyright © 2024 by Francoise Starks-Slaughter

Cover Design by MADDCity Media Group

Website: https://www.booksbyfrancoise.com

.This book was originally published by MADDCity Media Group

Francoise, Author

Ya'll Won't Let Me Sing: Chapter One by Francoise - First Edition

1. Children's book   2. Fiction   3. African American
4. Diversity   I. Francoise, authors   II. Title -Ya'll Won't Let Me Sing: Chapter One

Published by arrangement with MADDCity Media Group

All rights reserved.

Typeset Garamond

ISBN: 979-8-3304-6867-6

DEDICATION

To all the children around the world who have ever doubted themselves or questioned their ability to rise to any challenge—this is for you. May this story remind you that no matter how difficult something may seem, if you stay focused, determined, and believe in yourself, there is nothing you cannot achieve. You are capable of greatness, and your dreams are within reach. Keep striving, keep believing, and never let anything or anyone tell you otherwise.

CONTENTS

ACKNOWLEDGMENTS

I want to express my deepest gratitude to my loving husband for his unwavering support, and to my wonderful children, whose creativity continues to inspire me. To my parents, thank you for instilling in me the values of perseverance and faith. Lastly, to my childhood, which shaped me into who I am today, I am forever grateful for the lessons and love along the way.

CHAPTER ONE

In the year '77, a small baby named Franny was born. Franny had beautiful chocolate-brown eyes and lovely skin that made people want to eat her up, or at least that's what they always said.

As Fran got older, she had big, long, puffy ponytails that looked like they floated in the air when she played. She was the youngest of five kids and grew up in a musical family. Her cousins, aunt, and uncle were always around. Fran loved her family—they sang together, played the piano, guitar, and tambourine, and clapped their hands.

Every Sunday, they all went to church. Fran's mom and her sister sang together, and Fran loved hearing them sing. She always stood up in the front seat of the church, dreaming of singing with her family. One Sunday, at the age

of six, Fran stood up and said loudly,

"You didn't let me sing!" Her sisters laughed

and smiled at her.

Fran was shy and sang in a low tone with her

sisters at home while they practiced. When she

turned seven, she thought, "I am bigger now. I

know all the songs. I'm ready to sing at church

with my family." The week went by quickly, and

soon it was Sunday. Fran told herself, "This

Sunday is my chance."

She was nervous but found courage. She stood up in the front seat as usual and said, "Hey, I can sing!" But they just sat her down. She didn't understand why and felt sad with tears in her eyes. Throughout the week, Fran listened to her sisters practice and sang along with them until the next Sunday came. She said, "This time I'm going to put my favorite dress on."

Sunday came, and Fran sat in the front seat of the church again. When her mom and sisters began singing, she stood tall and said, "I can sing now," in a louder tone than before. Fran's mom picked her up, kissed her forehead, and smiled. But Fran wasn't happy. On Thursday night, she heard them practicing a song she loved and sang along with more effort.

When the third Sunday came, she said, "I'm going to put on my favorite dress and shoes." On Saturday night, she laid out her dress, shoes, and hair bow on her bed and went to sleep. Sunday arrived, and Fran sat in the front seat closer to her family. They began singing, and she stood up, singing part of the song strong and loud. Her mom smiled, and they continued to let Fran sing in the front with the family.

After church, the choir and Franny were happy. They cheered her on, shook her hand,

and said, "Good job, Fran." She spun around in her dress and said to her mom, "I finally got to sing in the church with you and my sisters." Her mom said, "Yes, great job, Fran."

Fran asked, "Can I sing by myself next time?" Her mom smiled and said, "Just practice your part with us for now." Fran said, "OK," but in her mind, she thought, "Sunday, I'm going to sing along. I want to be the big star."

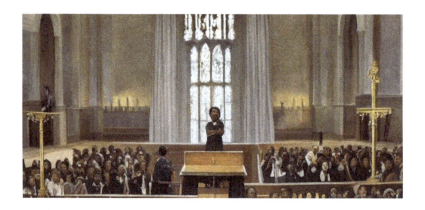

On the way home, Fran said to her mom, "I'm gonna be a big star one day." Her mom replied, "Yes, one day your time will come sooner than you think. Just practice every night." So, before bed, Fran and her mom sang a song together every night.

Her declaration: "My voice is a sound to change the atmosphere. I can sing loud and strong, soft and short, and long. I'm singing to help others feel good.

ABOUT THE AUTHOR

 Francoise, the author of the "Ya'll Won't Let Me Sing" book series, is a wife, mother, and daughter who works in the dental industry in Atlanta, Georgia. Born in Anderson, South Carolina, this is her first book series, and she considers it a true labor of love. Francoise poured her heart into creating these stories, hoping that children everywhere will enjoy and learn from them. Her message to all readers is that regardless of the color of your skin or any disability you may face, you can achieve anything you set your mind to. To learn more about the book series, contact her at fcarr53@gmail.com.

Printed in the USA
CPSIA information can be obtained
at www.ICGtesting.com
LVHW021159261124
797343LV00002B/27